Even MONSTERS say GOOD NIGHT

By Doreen Mulryan Marts

CAPSTONE YOUNG READERS

Published by
CAPSTONE YOUNG READERS
a Capstone imprint
1710 Roe Crest Drive
North Mankato, Minnesota 56003

www.capstoneyoungreaders.com

Library of Congress Cataloging-in-
Publication data is available on the
Library of Congress website.

ISBN: 978-1-62370-256-4 (hardcover)

Cover Vector: Shutterstock

Designer: K. Fraser

Printed in China.
032015   008858PettitF15

To my little girl, Avery, and your love of Halloween and questions.
Thank you for making the idea for this book possible!
– Mom

Avery never liked bedtime, and she liked it even less on Halloween when all the monsters were out.

Costume
ideas

Avery's mom tucked her into bed,
but Avery was NOT happy about it.
She knew there were monsters under
her bed, and probably in her closet, too.

Her mom explained that monsters sleep in their OWN beds in their OWN homes. Then she turned off the light and shut the door.

Avery thought about this, but she wasn't so sure.
She had a few more questions for her mom.

"Ghosts sleep in big haunted houses."

"Yes. They must go to bed the moment their potions are brewed for breakfast the next morning."

"Of course! They just sleep during the day instead of at night."

All the

Werewolves

Witches

Ghosts

Skeletons

Mummies

Vampires

are fast asleep, too.
Good night, my sweet girl.

So Avery went to bed,
but she still couldn't sleep.

She thought about all of the werewolves and witches
and ghosts and skeletons and mummies and vampires.

But Avery wasn't scared anymore.